Meet My

Written by Fay Robinson Ph

GoodYearBooks

My mouse has round, black eyes.
Like all mice, she has oval ears
and a pointed nose.

2

3

My mouse has brown and white spots.
Like all mice, she has very soft fur.

My mouse has long whiskers.
Like all mice, she uses her whiskers
to feel things around her.

6

My mouse has long teeth.
Like all mice, her teeth keep
growing. She chews things to keep
her teeth from growing too long.

9

My mouse has a long, thin tail.
Like all mice, her tail is as long
as her body.

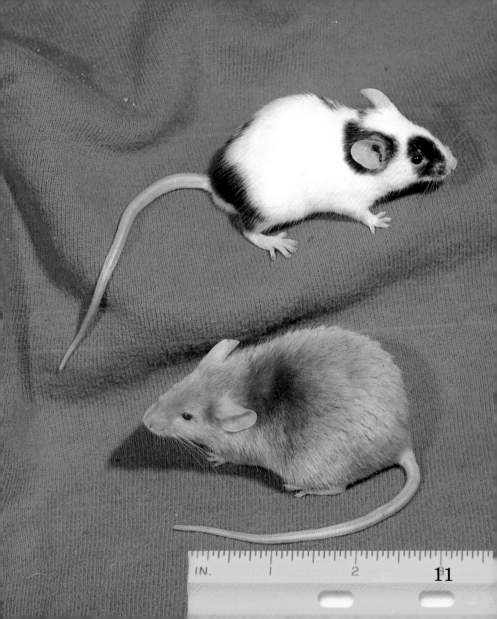

My mouse has lots to do.
Like all mice, she runs, climbs,
jumps, digs, and eats.

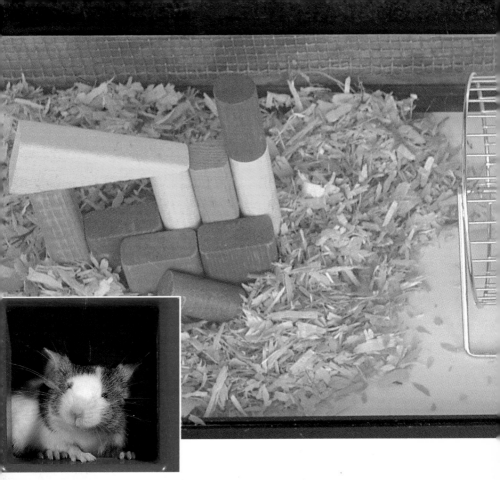

My mouse is a great pet.
Would you like a pet mouse?

You'll need a cage,
a water bottle, a food dish,
mouse food, litter, and . . .

your own mouse!

...ng with non-fiction, **Dianne Drake** penned ...reds of articles and seven books under the name ...pain. In 2001 she began her romance-writing ... with *The Doctor Dilemma*. In 2005 Dianne's ...Medical Romance, *Nurse in Recovery*, was ...shed, and with more than twenty novels to her ...t she has enjoyed writing ever since.

Also by Dianne Drake

Tortured by Her Touch
Doctor, Mummy...Wife?
The Nurse and the Single Dad
Saved by Doctor Dreamy
Bachelor Doc, Unexpected Dad

Sinclair Hospital Surgeons miniseries

Reunited with Her Army Doc
Healing Her Boss's Heart

Discover more at millsandboon.co.uk.